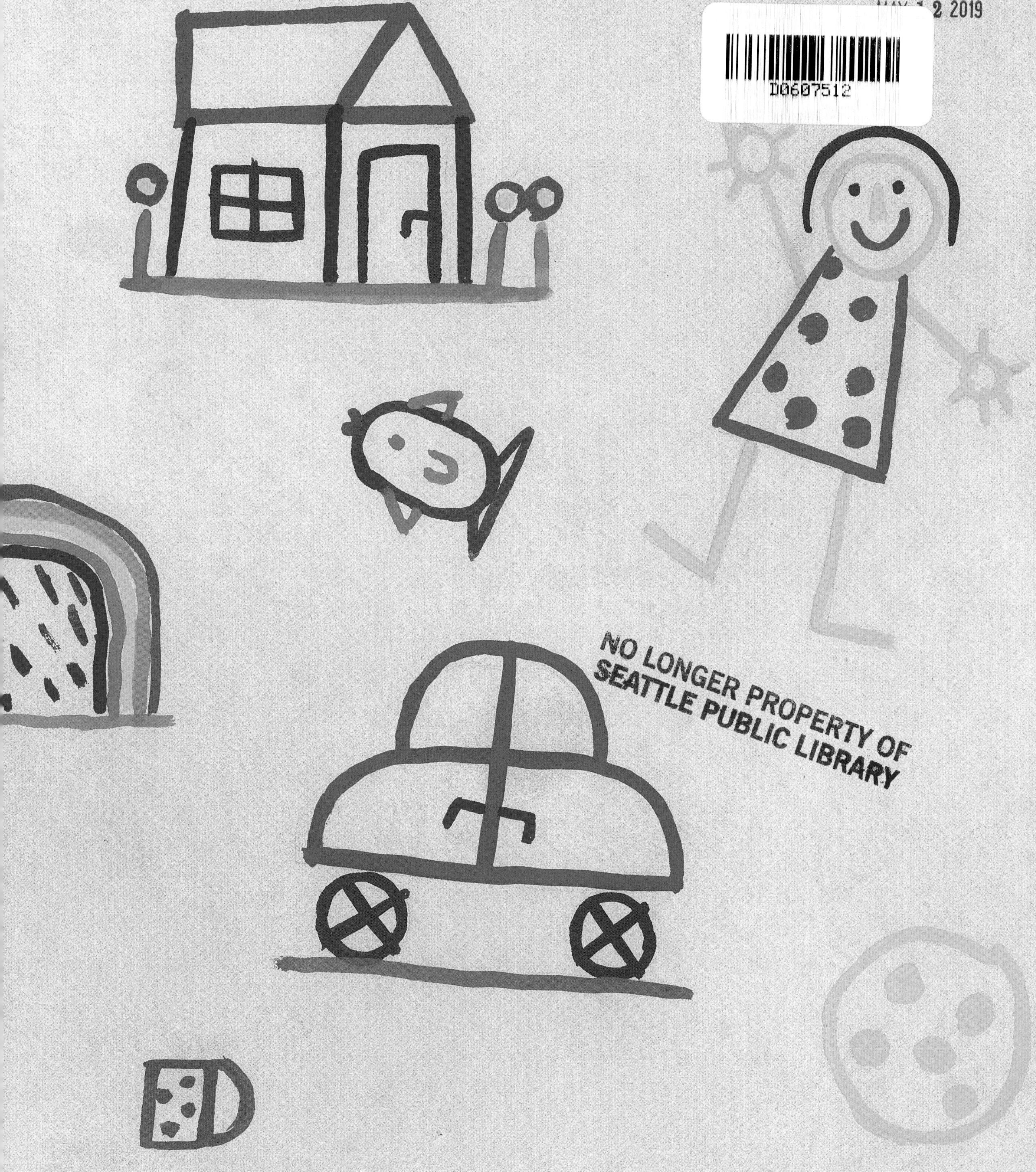

Paula Knows What to Do

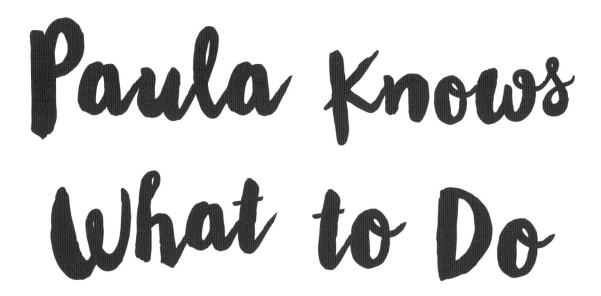

Sanne Dufft

pajamapress

First published in Canada and the United States in 2019

www.pajamapress.ca   info@pajamapress.ca

 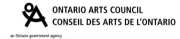

The publisher gratefully acknowledges the support of the Canada Council for the Arts and the Ontario Arts Council for its publishing program. We acknowledge the financial support of the Government of Canada through the Canada Book Fund (CBF) for our publishing activities.

Library and Archives Canada Cataloguing in Publication

Dufft, Sanne, 1974–, author, illustrator

    Paula knows what to do / Sanne Dufft.

ISBN 978-1-77278-068-0 (hardcover)

    I. Title.

PZ7.1.D84Pa 2019   j823'.92   C2018-903830-6

Publisher Cataloging-in-Publication Data (U.S.)

Names: Dufft, Sanne, 1974–, author.
Title: Paula Knows What to Do / Sanne Dufft.
Description: Toronto, Ontario Canada : Pajama Press, 2019. | Summary: "When Paula's father, grieving the loss of her mother, can't get out of bed one Saturday morning, Paula knows how to help him. She paints a picture and takes him on an imaginary journey until he feels well enough to take care of her in turn" – Provided by publisher.
Identifiers: ISBN 978-1-77278-068-0 (hardcover)
Subjects: LCSH: Parental grief – Juvenile fiction. | Care of the sick – Juvenile fiction. | Imagination – Juvenile fiction. | BISAC: JUVENILE FICTION / Social Themes / Death & Dying. | JUVENILE FICTION / Social Themes / Emotions & Feelings.
Classification: LCC PZ7.1D844Pa |DDC [F] – dc23

Original art created with watercolor
Cover and book design—Rebecca Bender

Manufactured by Qualibre Inc./Print Plus
Printed in China

Pajama Press Inc.
181 Carlaw Ave. Suite 251 Toronto, Ontario Canada, M4M 2S1

Distributed in Canada by UTP Distribution
5201 Dufferin Street Toronto, Ontario Canada, M3H 5T8

Distributed in the U.S. by Ingram Publisher Services
1 Ingram Blvd. La Vergne, TN 37086, USA

To my mother. And to my father, too.

There's something wrong today. Paula's daddy just stays in bed. No sound of bare feet on the wooden floor. No smell of coffee or hot chocolate.

Paula waits until she can't wait any longer.

Paula thinks, *I'll paint a picture for Daddy. He'll be up by the time I'm done.*

She paints a car. A fast one, with Daddy inside.

Daddy barely looks at it. He just stays in bed.

"It's Saturday," says Paula. "Aren't we reading a book this morning? Aren't you bringing my hot chocolate?"

"I don't know," Daddy says. "I can't get up just yet. I'm sad."

"Is it still because Mommy's gone?" asks Paula.

Her father nods.

Paula sighs. "I miss her too."

"I know what to do," says Paula. "Mommy loved to go sailing. Will you come sailing with me?"

"But, Paula," says Daddy. "I just want to stay in bed."

"*Nonsense*," says Paula (exactly the way Mommy used to say it). "We are going sailing. Mommy would want us to."

She gets a jar of water, a large sheet of paper, and some paints.

"Our boat is ready," says Paula.
It's time to set sail!"
   And off they go.
   It's a beautiful day. Sunny, with
just the right amount of wind.

Until...
"Oh no!" shouts Daddy.
"A storm!"

The wind howls and tears at the sail.

The waves are sky-high.

"I know what to do!"
Paula shouts.

"Help me with the sail!"
Quickly she unties the sail,
and they grab the ends.

The wind catches the
sail and carries them high
up into the sky.
"Daddy, we're flying!"

Paula and Daddy fly over vast fields,
high mountains, and steep canyons.

"And now what's happened?" Daddy asks.

"The wind has stopped," says Paula. "We must have fallen right onto your bed."

"Where's the sail?" Daddy asks.

"It's right here!"

Daddy nods. "I see. I thought this was my blanket."

"We're back," says Paula. "What now?"

This time, Daddy knows what to do.

"I'll make coffee for me and hot chocolate for you. But today, we don't need a book. We'll just look at your paintings again."

"Are you still sad, Daddy?"

"I am. But not as much. I'm so glad you knew what to do."

"So am I,"
says Paula.